"THE BUS STOP"

KYRO WAS EXCITED ABOUT GOING TO HIS NEW SCHOOL.

HIS OLDER BROTHER MARCO AND HIS OLDER SISTER MELANIN WERE ALREADY IN SCHOOL.

MARCO AND MELANIN WERE TWINS, AND THE TWINS WERE A YEAR OLDER THAN KYRO.

KYRO KNEW HE WOULD HAVE TO WAIT A WHOLE YEAR BEFORE HE COULD GO TO SCHOOL

WITH THEM.

EVERY MORNING THE TWINS WOULD GET DRESSED, PUT ON THEIR BOOKBAGS, PICK UP

THEIR LUNCH BOXES AND RUN OUTSIDE TO THE SCHOOL BUS. KYRO WOULD WATCH AS

ALL THE CHILDREN ON HIS BLOCK GATHERED AT THE BUS STOP.

SOME DAYS KYRO FELT SAD BECAUSE HE WAS MISSING OUT ON ALL THE COOL THINGS THAT THE TWINS COULD DO AT SCHOOL. KYRO WITNESSED MARCO PLAYING ON THE SCHOOL SOCCER TEAM WITH HIS CLEATS AND RED AND BLACK UNIFORM.

" MELANIN'S DANCE REHEARSAL "

Kyro also heard Melanin perform with the dance band; they all wore blue and gold glitter on their outfits. She had a cherry wood violin and also sang in the school chorus.

" THE HENDERSON CITY ZOO "

KYRO EVEN KNEW ABOUT THE TWINS GOING ON FIELD TRIPS IN SCHOOL TO THE ZOO, THE AQUARIUM, AND THE MUSEUM. KYRO WANTED TO GO SO BAD HE DECIDED TO ASK HIS DAD IF HE COULD GO.

" DADDY'S PLAYROOM "

KYRO'S DAD WOULD WAKE UP EVERY MORNING, MAKE BREAKFAST FOR HIMSELF, KYRO, AND THE TWINS AND THEN GO TO HIS PLAYROOM TO WORKOUT. DADDY'S PLAYROOM HAD A BIG PUNCHING BAG, HEAVY WEIGHTS, AND A JUMP ROPE. KYRO WAS NOT ALLOWED TO GO INTO DADDY'S PLAYROOM OR DISTURB HIM WHILE HE WAS LIFTING WEIGHTS, HOWEVER, HE WOULD WATCH THROUGH THE SCREEN IN THE DOOR TO SEE WHAT DAD WAS DOING. ONCE IN A WHILE, KYRO'S DAD WOULD TAKE HIM INSIDE TO LET HIM PLAY WITH THE JUMP ROPE AND BOXING GLOVES.

" **Do not be afraid to ask** "

KYRO DECIDED THAT HE WOULD CHANGE OUT OF HIS GRAY AND BLUE PAJAMAS AND PUT ON HIS LUCKY ORANGE SHIRT BEFORE ASKING DAD TO TAKE HIM ON THE SCHOOL TRIP. WHEN KYRO WAS TOLD THAT HE COULD NOT GO, KYRO DECIDED TO FIND ANOTHER WAY.

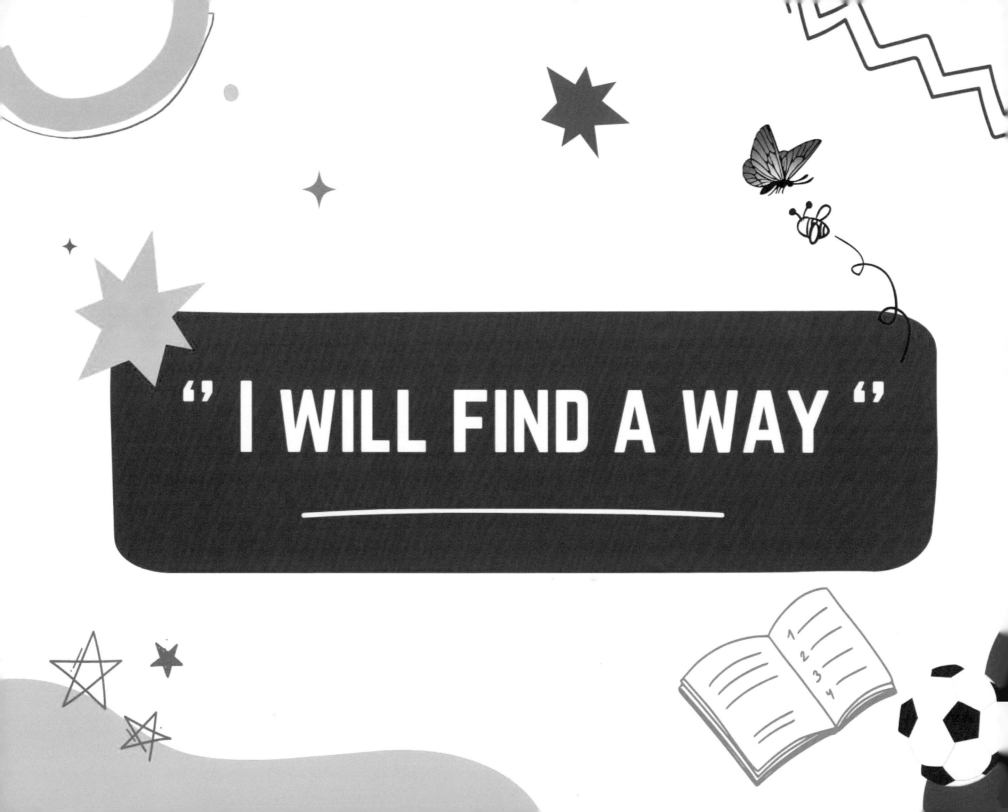

Kyro thought it was not fair that he could not play in the band, or join the soccer team. Kyro believed that he was good enough to play soccer and with the band. "And if I am good enough to play," he thought to himself, "Then I should be old enough to go."

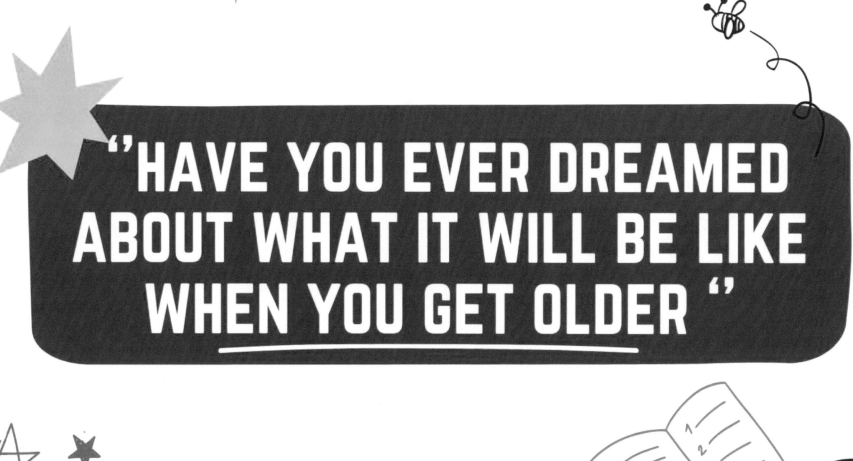

"HAVE YOU EVER DREAMED ABOUT WHAT IT WILL BE LIKE WHEN YOU GET OLDER "

That afternoon during nap time, Kyro closed his eyes and imagined himself being older than his big brother Marco and his big sister Melanin. What would it be like? What would he do? Where would he go? The longer he thought about it, the more he wanted to know. As he lay in bed something strange began to happen. Kyro began to grow.

When he opened his eyes he could hear the school bus rumbling outside. He ran to the door and saw Mr Moses, the bus driver waving to him. "Hi Kyro," Mr. Moses said, "Hop on the bus we are going to school." Kyro excitedly ran onto the bus and sat in a seat by the window. Kyro could feel the seats vibrating beneath his legs and smell the fumes from the engine as the bus took off rolling down the street.

KYRO GOT TO SCHOOL JUST AS MARCO AND THE SOCCER TEAM WERE BEGINNING TO PLAY. KYRO LOOKED DOWN AND SAW HE HAD ON THE FRESH NEW CLEATS AND THE RED AND BLACK UNIFORM. HE RAN ON THE FIELD AND KICKED THE BALL HIGH IN THE AIR, LANDING INSIDE THE NET FOR THE SCORE. KYRO WON THE GAME! HIS FRIENDS AND TEAMMATES PICKED HIM UP AND CARRIED HIM OFF THE FIELD, CELEBRATING.

AFTER SCHOOL, THE STUDENTS GATHERED INTO THE AUDITORIUM TO HEAR THE BAND PLAY. THEY INVITED KYRO ON STAGE TO AWARD HIM FOR WINNING THE GAME. KYRO LOVED THE SOUNDS OF ALL THE MUSICAL INSTRUMENTS. SO THEY LET HIM PLAY WHATEVER HE LIKED. KYRO PICKED UP A VIOLIN. KYRO'S SISTER, MELANIN, HAD HER VIOLIN AS WELL, AND THEY BOTH WORE THE BLUE AND GOLD GLITTERED HATS. AS THE TWO OF THEM PLAYED SONGS TOGETHER AND DANCED, THE TEACHERS AND STUDENTS CHEERED.

There was one thing left for Kyro that would make his day complete. He had gone to school, rode a school bus, won a soccer game and jammed with the band. What else could Kyro want to do? Kyro wanted to sneak into Dad's workout room to play with the boxing gloves, but the door was locked and Kyro knew where to find a key. It was above the door frame, where he could not reach. All he had to do was climb up to grab it. Kyro knew that he was taller than he was before and he thought, "If I am tall enough to get in, I should be old enough to go in." During his climb, Kyro fell.

When he woke, Kyro had on his lucky orange shirt. He saw his gray and blue pajamas in the clothes basket where he had left them. He did not have on the new cleats. He did not wear a red and black uniform or any blue and gold hats. All Kyro had was a dream. A very good one Kyro admitted.

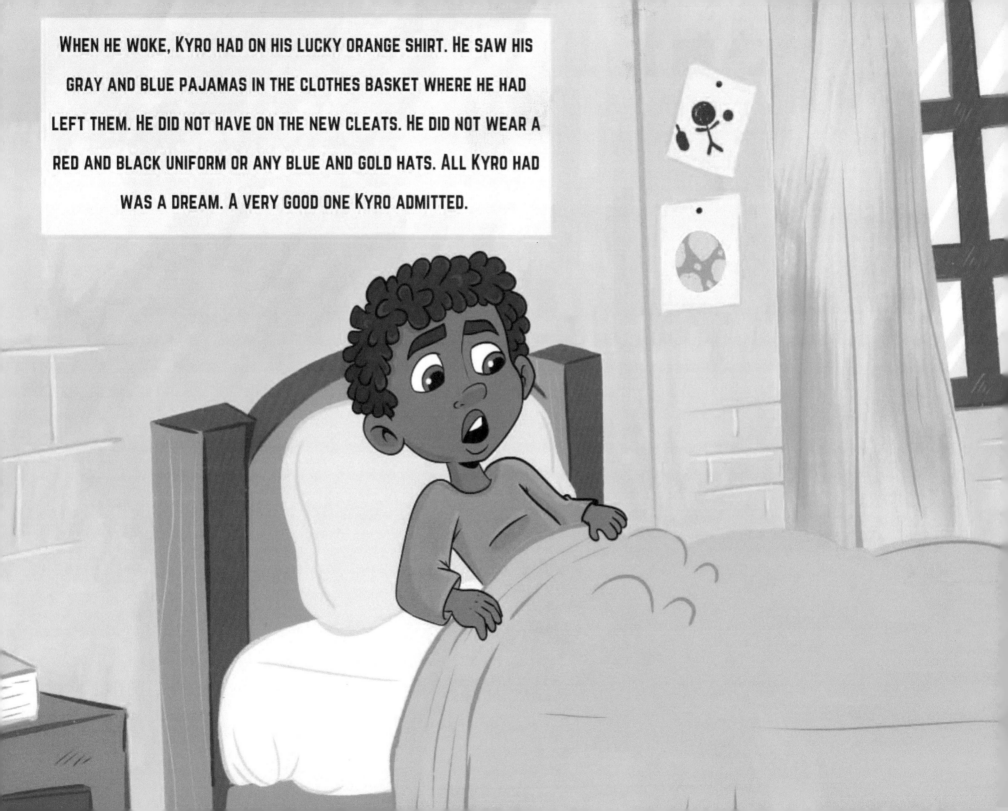

But just as Kyro started to rise from his nap, he heard his mom and the twins come home. "Daddy, where are my soccer shoes?" Marco yelled. Kyro thought about his soccer dream and smiled. "Mom, have you seen my violin?" Melanin asked. Kyro remembered his violin performance with pride. Then Kyro's Dad called out, "Honey, have you seen my boxing gloves?"

WHEN KYRO HEARD THIS, HE JUST SMILED, ROLLED OVER AND PRETENDED THAT HE WAS STILL SLEEPING.

"THE END"

CPSIA information can be obtained
at www.ICGtesting.com
Printed in the USA
BVRC100838020522
635884BV00003B/10